your very own special

Bucks the Palace Cat

written by

Stuart James

with

Bucks the Palace Cat was written by Stuart James who owns the copyright © 2020.
First published in 2020 by The Happily Ever Press. Pictures by You is an imprint of The Happily Ever Press.

This story is also available in other formats.

No part of this publication may be reproduced, stored in or introduced into a retrieval system,
or transmitted, in any form, or by any means (electronic, mechanical, photocopying, recording
or otherwise) without the prior written permission of the copyright owner or publisher.

ISBN: 979-8-66360-201-3

Welcome to this very special edition of

Bucks the Palace Cat

in which you can use your own imagination
to make a book unique to you. This is
the complete version of the children's story.
All that is missing are the pictures!
And that's where **you** come in. Look out for the
empty frames throughout this book and use paints,
crayons, collage or whatever you like to make
your pictures. You could even create 3D scenes,
photograph them, then stick in the photos!
There are 10 empty frames inside to fill with

pictures by YOU

tip If you are using paints or anything sticky to
make your pictures, it might be better to do them on a
separate piece of paper and stick them in when dry.
The space inside the frame is about A5 size
(that's half A4). But you could make a picture
as big as you like, photograph it, print it out
at a smaller size and stick it in!

✳

Enjoy the story and have fun
making your pictures!

You could always add some doodles around the pages too

This book has been illustrated by ...

· ·

The characters

Why not create portraits of our two heroes, Bucks and Private Jones

Bucks

Pte. Jones

It was an ordinary day,
well, as ordinary
as a day at the Palace can be.

The flag flew high
which meant the Queen was inside –
going about "One's" Royal Routine.

With the Queen being at home,
of course everyone
was on their very best form –
from the Duke to the Cook,
Head Gardener to the Footman,
to the ladies and men
of The Guard ...

... and even the furry black cat
they called Bucks
was quietly curled up in the yard.

Left right left right ...
Through a half-opened eye
Bucks watched the soldiers
of The Guard march by.

Then he rested his chin
on his paws once again
and he purred and he yawned
and he happily sighed.

Today, surely no one
would step out of line.
Everything at Buckingham Palace
would be fine.

A crowd by now

had gathered

outside the Palace gates.

They waved their flags

as the sun shone down.

It was the perfect day

to see

THE CHANGING OF THE GUARD

Now, The Guard,

are the brave ladies and men

who serve to protect the Palace

and Queen.

And as well as looking

impeccably smart

'Alert at all times'

they must be.

So at eleven o'clock,
or thereabouts most days,
the Old Guard
and the New Guard
come together and change.

The Old Guard march out.
Left right left right ...
and the New Guard march in.
Right left right left ...

It's a parade that simply must be
one of Britain's Greatest traditions.
The colour! The pomp!
The majesty! ...
A quite splendid occasion.

But for one young Private
from the Valleys,
named Jones,
it was an extra special day ...
His first
serving country and Queen
and he could barely wait.

He'd brushed his red jacket,
shone the brass buttons,
polished his boots til they gleamed.
He'd ironed his trousers
and even his socks ...
and his teeth had never been so clean!

Like his first day at school
he felt proud and excited ...
and a butterfly flew round in his tum.
But he thought of a lady
back home in Wales
so proud to be his mum.

In the distance a big clock
called Big Ben chimed ten
as the captain yelled out
"Ready ladies and men!"
Young Private Jones
straightened his collar again
and joined
the back of the line.

However ...
he had a rather bad feeling
that he'd gone and
left something behind.

Meanwhile back at the Palace,
Bucks was dutifully washing his face.
He preened and groomed.
And groomed and preened,
leaving no hair out of place.
Well it just wouldn't do
for a Royal cat to
bring upon the Palace
disgrace.

So properly presented,
his chores all completed
with no rats or mice left to catch,
Bucks slunk off
to inspect The New Guard
and ensure they were all
up to scratch.

You see,
Bucks had quite a critical eye –
no scuffed cuff
or lace untied
or even a loose thread went by
without a glower
or a stare.

But today those keen, discerning eyes
could not find anything awry
as he strutted his way along the line
a few paces ahead of the Captain;
right to the end
where our friend, Private Jones,
was standing ...

Jones looked at Bucks.

Bucks looked at Jones.

Bucks looked at Jones again.

Then blinked ...

Once ...

Twice ...

This couldn't be right.

Were his eyes deceiving him?

Then suddenly the shock became

just too much to bear.

His eyes widened like saucers.

His body launched into the air.

From a calm, composed, cool cat burst

a spiky ball of fur,

fizzing like a 'cat'herine wheel,

a hairy, black explosion ...

For there in line, looking back,

was a Private

with no hat on!

No hat!
This cat
could not have that.
He sprang right into action.
And in a flash
quick-thinking Bucks …
was on top of Jones's head,
in fact
forming quite the perfect dome
– and just in time
as it turned out –
as the Captain stopped
and said …
"Very smart, Jones. Well done,"
before ordering,
"Guard …
March on!"

Well, that short walk from the Barracks
to the Palace felt like one
of the longest marches Jones had ever made …
nervous that his make-do hat –
his living, breathing feline hat –
should suddenly decide to go astray.

Birdcage Walk was particularly tense
when a pigeon whistled past Bucks's ear,
then a busker's dog seemed to catch the scent of 'mog'
and barked and barked but Bucks betrayed no fear.
Even 'Big Jim's Big Fish Van' didn't
wrinkle Bucks's nose,
not even with a two-for-one
on 'Plaice and Chips to go.'

Bucks the Palace cat
resolutely sat,
the honour of the country in his paws.
Not a muscle moved.
Nor a whisker twitched.
He kept his shape
and basked in the applause.

No one seemed to notice in the crowd,
well, no one said,
"Look, that soldier, last in line
has got a cat upon his head."

So the Guard marched on
to waves and cheers
through the Palace Gates ...
Left. Right. Left. Right
Left 'til "Halt!"

They stopped to face
the soldiers of the Old Guard
whom they would soon replace.

And as the band played
a rousing tune,
soldiers Old and New,
raised their rifles,
presented arms,
and
FIRED
a royal salute!

Then as the captain
of the Old Guard
gave the captain of the New
the key to the Palace,
Jones looked up
and whispered "Phew!"
"That was close
That was hairy.
Why thanks, puss,
you've gone and saved me
from a whole heap of trouble
to be sure."

But then Bucks began to fidget.
Jones implored "Just a few more minutes!"
But Bucks's senses were on 'high alert'.
It started with a sniff,
a sniff that'd caught a whiff,
a whiff of something fishy in the air.
Bucks opened half an eye ...
Then the other. Then he spied
something not quite right
over there ...

Jones by now had also seen
a man from the crowd break free,
scale the railings
and land inside ...
inside the Palace grounds!

And more than that ...
the man was armed!
He brandished a baguette
and as he ran towards the Palace,
Bucks did quite forget
his role as Private Jones's hat.
Once again he was a cat –
a loyal, trusty cat whose job
was to defend
his Palace home.

"Friend or foe?"
a sentry yelled,
as from Jones's shoulders
Bucks leaped down
and gave frantic chase.

So this was the scene
that greeted the Queen,
looking out of the drawing room window:
A man with a baguette
being chased by a cat,
who in turn
was pursued by a
a Guard with no hat!
I say ...
It was enough
to spill one's Earl Grey.
(And she did).

Panic had rippled
right through the ranks
and the crowd all clamoured to see.
As the cat gathered pace
in a furious race,
the Captain cried,
"Bucks! Save The Queen!"

The intruder by now
was yards from the door ...
Then Jones recalled his rugby at school –
He'd been the fastest flanker they'd known –
in a sudden burst of pace,
he'd made up the ground
and just as the bread-wielding rogue
turned around,
Jones looked at Bucks ...
Bucks looked at Jones.
Together they pounced ...
and brought the man down.

And before you could say
"Where's that Guard's hat?"
the man was disarmed
by an extraordinary cat,
with an extraordinary
liking for tuna!

Then ...
"Daddy. Daddy," a small voice cried out,
and everyone looked around
to see a little girl in a pretty blue dress
had shyly emerged from the crowd.

"Oh sweetheart, I'm sorry, what have I done?"
said the man lying down on the ground.
"I must apologise to everyone.
I really didn't mean any harm.
I was just chasing after my daughter's balloon –
she'd let go when she'd jumped
when they fired the salute.
I know I've done wrong. I've been such a fool.
But it was the last one they had at the stall
and I didn't want to let her down."

"Well, at least the Queen's safe,"
said the Captain,
breathing a sigh of relief.

"Oh no she's not," said Jones, pointing up
and all eyes now turned to the roof
where Her Royal Highness appeared to be stuck
holding a child's balloon.
"Don't worry, m'am,
we'll soon have you down,"
said the Captain.
(And so they did).

The balloon was returned
to a grateful young girl;
her dad received a Royal Pardon,
then all were invited to lunch
with the Queen
and the Duke
in the Palace Gardens.

Later that year, Private Jones was knighted.
His mum, of course, thrilled to be there,
remembered a boy whose favourite toy
was a wooden soldier he'd won at the fair.

As for Bucks, that most extraordinary cat,
he was awarded an F.O.B.E* –
which basically meant the odd Royal favour
and the finest tuna for tea.

And as cats will do,
he'll take the odd liberty.
In fact I've heard it said ...

Sshhh ...

When the flag flies low and the Queen's away,
he'll take his nap
On Her Majesty's bed.

The End

* Feline Order of the British Empire – an award recognising cats who have
demonstrated services to their country above and beyond the call of duty.
(Someone might have made that up).

I hope you have enjoyed making your
very own, truly unique edition of this story!
I would love to see your finished books, so feel
free to send photos to my email address at
mybucksthepalacecat@thehappilyeverpress.uk
Of course, ask a grown up first! I might even
put some on the website if that is ok.

Bucks the Palace Cat
is also available in other formats.

Thank you for buying or borrowing this book.
Look out for news and future stories by Stuart James at
TheHappilyEverPress.uk
I hope to release other **pictures by you** books soon.

Stuart

© TheHappilyEverPress.uk

Printed in Great Britain
by Amazon

46027946R00020